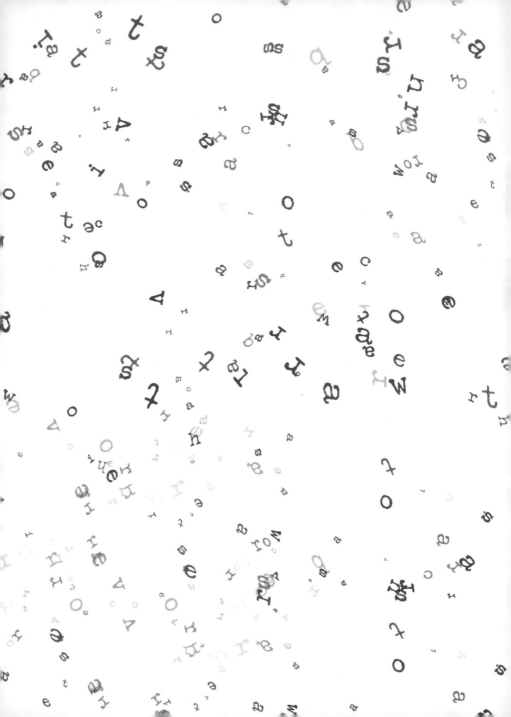

ghost writer™

Published by Sourcebooks Wonderland, an Imprint of Sourcebooks Kids.
Sourcebooks and the colophon are registered trademarks of Sourcebooks.
All Rights Reserved.
P.O. Box 4410, Naperville, Illinois 60567-4410
(630) 961-3900
Fax: (630) 961-2168
sourcebooks.com

sesameworkshop.org

Design by Whitney Manger
Recipe and Brainteaser illustrations by Jenny Bee

Library of Congress data is on file with the publisher.

Printed and bound in the United States of America.
MA 10 9 8 7 6 5 4 3 2 1

ghost writer™

TRINITY

WITHDRAWN

by D. J. MacHale

with an introduction by Kwame Alexander

sourcebooks
wonderland

SESAME WORKSHOP.

Dear Rock Star Reader,

Books are like amusement parks, and this one here is a roller coaster. As you begin your reading adventure, I just want to chime in and say get ready for an incredibly amazing experience reimagining some of your favorite books. That's right: between the pages of this book, Ghostwriter is bringing your favorite characters to life to help solve a mystery. How cool is that?

I bet you think that because I'm an author, I love to read. Well, you're right! In order to become a good writer, you gotta be a great reader. Every time you read a meaningful or magical poem or story or really clever post, you're instantly transformed and sometimes transported to new ideas and worlds: sports arenas, foreign lands, outer space, other times in history, and even other kids' lives. But I wasn't always that way.

When I was twelve, I thought reading was uncool. Why? Because my dad chose huge, boring books he thought

I should read. After a few years of that torture, my mom encouraged me to pick out my own books at our local library, and I found my way back to finding reading cool. (I guess you could say I started choosing my own rides at the amusement park.) Then I started reading everything—chapter books, short stories, comic books, biographies, and, of course, poetry. Ghostwriter, like my mom, believes that there's a perfect book for every kid out there. And the one you're reading could be yours.

I love getting lost in a good story, and there are so, so many great stories out there just waiting for you. Our friend Ghostwriter is gonna help you find them—and then rock your world one page at a time.

I thank you for your attention, and I'm outta here!

Kwame Alexander

Poet, Educator, and Newbery Medal–winning author of *The Crossover*

chapter 1

The kid looked scared.

He charged into the town of Silver Spur, holding tight to the worn leather saddle for fear he might be slung from his powerful ride. A cloud of brown dust kicked up everywhere. It clung to his white shirt and white cowboy hat as he flew along Main Street, looking for help.

Silver Spur was a sleepy little Western town with wooden sidewalks and dirt streets. There was a blacksmith shop, a general store, an undertaker's parlor, a feed and grain store, and, halfway to the far end, the Mine Car Hotel. The hotel was the most inviting building on Main Street. It gleamed with a fresh coat of dazzling blue paint and was trimmed by white windows and balconies. It stood out like a special birthday gift next to the drab wooden buildings on either side of it.

Happy sounds of music and laughter from within drew the kid to it like a thirsty traveler headed for a bubbling spring of fresh water. He brought his ride to a quick stop in front. Jumping out of the saddle, he sprinted toward the sounds of life.

He pushed open the front door and looked

around. Several wooden tables scattered throughout the lobby were filled with cowboys playing cards, gobbling down beans and crusty bread, and singing. A layer of brown dust covered each and every one of the men, as if they'd just come in from a cattle drive. A frazzled waiter rushed from table to table, keeping the hungry cowboys' plates filled. A player piano pounded out a rollicking tune.

A splendid time was being had by all.

Except for the kid. He wasn't happy at all.

He ran to the front desk, scanning about for the hotel clerk. His gaze traveled over an elaborate array of items decorating the shelves behind the counter. He saw sepia-toned photos of miners, stuffed and mounted trophy heads of various-sized elk, and brass bowls filled with beef jerky and hard-boiled eggs. In the dead center, an impressive baseball-size chunk of silver ore rested on a purple pillow.

The kid's eyes grew wide when he spotted the prize.

"Lookin' for a room, young fella?" The hotel clerk strolled out from a back room behind the counter. He was nearly bald and his handlebar mustache drooped down either side of his mouth, then curled up like a double smile.

"Don't need no room," the kid said, breathless. "I need the sheriff."

"Sheriff?" the clerk said with a chuckle. "Ain't no sheriff in Silver Spur. Ain't no *crime* in Silver Spur."

"What happens when there *is* a crime?" the kid asked.

"A marshal comes through every so often," he said with a shrug. "Mostly to say howdy and to grab a hot meal. Like I said, ain't no crime in Silver Spur."

"Until now," the kid said. "I need help."

The clerk frowned. He looked the kid up and down, trying to decide if he should be taken seriously.

"You stay right there, young fella." He turned and leaned into the doorway he'd entered through, and called, "You might want to take a look at this."

A moment later, a woman wearing a blue-and-white-checkered dress and a well-worn apron stepped out of the back room and dried her hands on a towel. She had the focused look of someone who had a lot of chores to do and didn't appreciate being bothered. The clerk gestured to the kid and whispered something to the woman. She glanced at the young visitor, who was now sitting up on the counter with his legs dangling down. She raised her eyebrows.

"We got chairs for sitting," she said with a no-nonsense attitude that proved she was the boss of the Mine Car Hotel.

The kid jumped off quickly. "Sorry, ma'am."

"My clerk says you came charging in here all fired up about some crime being committed. That right?"

"Sure is."

"What's your name?"

"They call me the Camarillo Kid."

"Oh, do they?" the woman said with a grin. "A handle like that usually comes with a reputation. What's yours?"

"Ain't got no reputation, ma'am. Just a heap of trouble."

"You can call me Scarlett," she said, warming up to him. "Tell me what happened."

"It's my folks," he blurted out. "We were passing through south of here and got jumped by a desperado. He kidnapped Ma and Pa and told me to bring him a hundred dollars or there's no telling what he might do to them."

Scarlett glanced at the hotel clerk with concern.

He shrugged. He didn't know what to make of the story.

"Did you get the name of this desperado?" she asked the Kid.

"I did! He said his name was Hitch."

Scarlett frowned. "Never heard of him. Where are you supposed to meet this Hitch to bring him the money?"

"A place called Desperation Gulch. You heard of it?"

"Of course. It's on the far side of Shadow Gap. About a few hours' ride from here."

"Is that the same Shadow Gap that's got a gold mine in it?" the Kid asked.

"It is, and it's a dangerous trip. It's no place for a pup like you," said Scarlett.

"Don't matter none. I gotta go and save Ma and Pa," insisted the Kid.

"Where you goin' to get a hundred dollars?"

The Kid leaned close to Scarlett and whispered, "Already got it. We had the money all along. We would've given it to him if we knew what he was fixin' to do, but once he rode off with my folks, it was too late."

"Well now, Camarillo Kid, I'm thinking you should wait for the marshal to get here."

"When's that?"

"Couple of days."

"Couple of days!" the Kid cried. "My folks could be buzzard food by then!"

The lobby fell quiet. The cowboys stopped what they were doing to stare at the Kid.

"You all mind your own business," Scarlett called out, scolding the room.

The cowboys went back to their food and card games.

"Can you direct me to Shadow Gap?" the Kid asked.

Scarlett hesitated. The Kid was young, but he wasn't a little boy. He looked to be about fourteen…old enough to know what he was doing.

"Keep riding north out of town," she said. "When the road forks, head West toward the mountains. You'll hit Shadow Gap soon enough. But like I said, it's dangerous. You really should wait for the marshal."

"Can't do that." The Kid raced across the lobby, dodging tables, headed for the front door.

Once outside, he made straight for his ride.

Scarlett watched through the grimy front window as the Kid jumped into the saddle. He sped off, charging after a kidnapping desperado named Hitch.

"Good luck, Camarillo Kid," Scarlett called out. "I'm afraid you're going to need it."

chapter 2

The Camarillo Kid was well on his way to Desperation Gulch when a second stranger arrived in Silver Spur. This man came in on foot.

He looked to have been through some pretty rough times for someone not much older than twenty years old. The stubble of a beard meant he hadn't shaved in a week. The layer of grime on his dark clothes hinted at troubles he'd seen on the trail. His dark cowboy hat was pulled low over his watchful eyes, making it hard for anybody to see what he was looking at. Or whom.

He walked slowly down the center of Main Street, his boots kicking up dirt. The lazy drag in his step signalled he might be exhausted, hurt, or in desperate need of water. Maybe all three.

The people of Silver Spur took one look at him and hurried inside, locking their doors. He stalked to the center of town, oblivious to the riders on horseback steering clear of him. He stopped, gazed around thoughtfully, and spotted the Mine Car Hotel. The music drew him in, just as it had the Camarillo Kid.

He pushed open the door, and the place instantly fell quiet. Card games stopped. So did the laughing and singing. The only sound that didn't stop was the music from the player piano. The dangerous-looking stranger was not a welcome sight in the peaceful town of Silver Spur.

If being stared at bothered the man, he didn't show it. He strode slowly through the lobby, ignoring the cowboys who followed him with wary eyes. He headed for the front desk. The clerk stood behind it, nervously drumming his fingers on the countertop.

Scarlett watched from the doorway to the back room. The hotel clerk's eyes grew wide with fear as the stranger moved closer. They locked gazes for several seconds before the clerk spoke.

"Hello, friend," he said, his voice cracking. "You need food or a room?"

"Neither. I'm looking for a boy. 'Bout fourteen," the stranger said in a low, husky voice that sounded like he hadn't had a drink of water in a week.

"Seems like you need to wet your whistle." The clerk poured a glass of water from a pitcher.

The stranger took the glass. Without a word, he downed every last drop in one huge gulp. The clerk shot a nervous look at Scarlett. She nodded, and the clerk filled the glass again. The stranger downed this second glass as quickly as the first, then wiped his mouth on his sleeve.

"Much obliged," he said. The scratchy rasp in his voice was gone. He glanced over his shoulder at the cowboys staring at him.

"I was a might thirsty," he announced to the room.

The cowboys quickly went back to their business. They didn't want anything to do with the man in the black hat.

Scarlett walked up to the stranger and looked him square in the eyes. "You say you're looking for a boy?"

"I am." The man gave a polite tip of his hat. "Leonard's his name."

"A youngster came through about an hour or so back," Scarlett said. "Called himself the Camarillo Kid."

"That's him," the stranger said with a snicker. "At least I believe that's what he's calling himself now."

"And who might you be?" Scarlett asked boldly.

"The name's Hitchcock. Most call me Hitch. Do you know where the boy's at?"

Scarlett gave a slight nod to someone behind Hitch. Hitch saw this and spun around too late. Three cowboys jumped him and pinned his arms to the counter. Hitch didn't fight back. It was three on one.

Scarlett leaned in. "Ain't no crime in Silver Spur and we don't plan on letting any in."

"That's awful noble of you, ma'am," Hitch said calmly.

Scarlett's eye caught something on Hitch's shirt underneath his dark jacket. She reached out and flipped the collar aside to reveal...a gleaming silver marshal's badge.

"You're a marshal?" she asked with surprise.

"I am."

"What's a marshal doing kidnapping innocent folks and holding 'em for ransom?" she demanded.

"Is that what Leonard told you?" Hitch said. "Don't surprise me none. Let me tell you something about that fine, upstanding young man.

He's a thief. And a liar. And those are the good things I can say about him. I've been tracking him for days. I was getting close, but then last night, when I was sleeping on the trail, he stole my gear and my water, and made off with Patches."

"Patches?" the clerk asked.

"Sweetest ride I ever had. Now she's gone. He left me out in the desert to roast. I've been walking in the hot sun for hours, following his trail."

"That sweet little boy did that?" Scarlett asked.

"He may be a little boy, but there ain't nothing sweet about him," Hitch said. "Fact is, I've known him since he was just a squirt. I guess that's why they sent me out looking for him. I know how he thinks."

"Do you?" the clerk said with a laugh. "Then how come you didn't guess he was going to steal your ride and all your gear?"

Hitch shot the man a quick, angry look.

The clerk stopped laughing.

Then Hitch smiled and said, "Yeah, I reckon maybe you're right about that."

The clerk let out a relieved breath.

"Why should we believe you?" Scarlett asked. "It's your word against his."

"My guess is if you had the pleasure of Leonard's company, he took something from you, too. He can't help himself. It's what he does," said Hitch.

"He didn't take anything," Scarlett said. "If he had, I'd surely know—"

"The Madre!" the clerk exclaimed.

The clerk pointed to the purple pillow behind the front counter that held the large chunk of silver ore. Or that *used* to hold it. The pillow was empty. The clerk picked it up and shook it angrily.

"The Madre was the biggest chunk of silver ever dug around these parts," he cried. "One of a kind!"

"And now it's gone," Hitch said matter-of-factly. "Don't surprise me none. Like I said, it's what he does."

"Let him go," Scarlett commanded the three cowboys.

The cowboys let go of Hitch, who tipped his hat to them. "Much obliged, gentlemen. No hard feelings."

The cowboys gathered around the clerk, who held the purple pillow. They all stared at it, as if hoping the silver ore would magically appear.

It didn't.

"This is horrible." Scarlett moaned. "That silver was going to pay for the church we were fixing to build. The people of this town have been doing without one for years. There's no way we can pay for it without the money we'd get from selling the Madre."

"Don't you worry," Hitch said. "I'll track Leonard down and get your silver back. You'll have your church."

"How?" the clerk demanded. "You don't even have a ride!"

"Right." Hitch scratched his chin thoughtfully. "I'll need to work on that."

"The Kid said he was headed for Desperation Gulch," Scarlett said.

"That's through Shadow Gap," Hitch added. "There's a gold mine in there, if I remember correctly."

"There is," the clerk said. "Gilroy's gold mine. He laid claim to it years ago."

"It's dangerous going through the gap,"

Scarlett said. "You should deputize some of our fine men here and bring 'em along for protection."

Hitch took a quick look around at the room. A dozen cowboys seemed eager to go after the thief who'd stolen their silver.

"I appreciate that," Hitch said. "But I work alone. Always have. I will be needing supplies, though."

He reached into his pocket, pulled out several gold coins, and tossed them onto the counter. "Can somebody fix me up?"

"I can oblige you with that," came a voice from the front door.

Several cowboys stepped out of the way to reveal a man dressed all in black. A thick mustache covered his entire mouth, and long, greasy hair fell to his shoulders. He held a coil of rope in one hand. In the other hand, he held the lasso end of the rope. He swung it back and forth menacingly.

"Howdy, Rangel," Hitch said, greeting the man.

"You know this fella?" Scarlett asked with surprise.

"We've crossed paths."

"Howdy to you, Marshal," the man in black said coldly. "Been looking for you for quite some time. Thought I'd never catch up with you. Then I came across a kid who said I'd find you here."

"Lucky me," Hitch said. "What can I do for you?"

"We got us a score to settle," said Rangel.

"Don't surprise me none. I put Mr. Rangel behind bars a while back for cattle rustling. He's quite handy with that lasso," Hitch told Scarlett.

"Yes, I am." Rangel swung the noose higher.

"Seems as though Mr. Rangel is holding a grudge," Hitch said.

"No grudge," Rangel said. "I just want me some payback, is all."

"Sounds like a grudge to me," Hitch said.

The tension in the lobby was thick. Nobody moved.

"I'm a fair man," Rangel said. "I'll make you an offer. We'll have a contest. If you win, you can take my horse and all my gear."

"And if *you* win?" Hitch asked.

"Then I get all your gold and, best of all, you'll be six feet under."

Hitch thought for a moment and nodded. "Sounds fair. What's the contest?"

Rangel spun the noose end of the rope out in front of him, creating a circle in the air. He was definitely an expert with the rope.

"I'll be the rustler," Rangel said. "You be the steer. Contest is, you try to keep from getting strung up."

Hitch shook his head "Not sure I like that particular contest—"

Before he could say another word, Rangel flung the lasso at him, forcing the cowboys between them to dive out of the way.

Hitch thought fast and grabbed one of the chairs from under a table. He held it upside down over his head, and the noose circled the chair's legs, rather than Hitch's neck.

Rangel yanked back on the rope, tightening the loop around the chair's legs.

He pulled hard.

Hitch pulled harder. He jerked the chair back, knocking Rangel off balance. Rangel stumbled forward, but he held tight to the rope.

That was all the time Scarlett needed. She quickly grabbed a heavy plate full of beans off a table and threw it at Rangel. The plate spun through the air, spewing beans everywhere. It clipped Rangel in the forehead, sending him reeling backward.

And he let go of the rope.

Hitch looked up and spotted a wooden beam overhead. He threw the chair up, looping the rope that was attached to it over the top of the beam.

Rangel got his wits back quickly and dove for his end of the rope.

Too late. The chair fell back down. Hitch caught it, and now he held both ends of the rope.

Rangel let out an angry cry and charged for Hitch.

He didn't get far before the hotel clerk tackled him. The two crashed to the floor, and the clerk sat on his chest.

"Ain't no crime in Silver Spur, and we ain't having any now," the clerk said.

With the skill of an expert rodeo cowboy, Hitch quickly trussed up Rangel's ankles. "Pull!" he shouted to the cowboys.

Two men grabbed the other end of the rope and pulled, hand over hand, lifting Rangel into the air by his ankles. The cattle rustler hung there, swaying back and forth, helpless.

Hitch caught his breath and walked up to him. They were face-to-face, with Rangel upside down.

"Looks like I win the contest, Mr. Rangel," Hitch said.

"I truly hate you, Hitchcock," Rangel said through gritted teeth.

"You're not the only thief who's told me that," Hitch said with a smile. "Just means I'm doing my job. Now, if you don't mind, I'll be collecting my winnings."

A few minutes later, Hitch was mounted on Rangel's golden palomino named Casey. Rangel's lasso was coiled up and strapped to the saddle. Scarlett and the hotel clerk stood next to Hitch.

"Please find that lyin' thief, Marshal," she said. "I can't tell you how valuable the Madre is to our town. We need you to bring it back."

"That's exactly what I aim to do, ma'am." He touched the brim of his hat, tipping it to her politely. "Thank you kindly for the information, and for helping me out with Mr. Rangel. Never thought a dinner plate could do so much damage."

"It's one less dish I have to wash!" The clerk laughed.

"We'll untie Rangel and hold on to him until the next marshal comes through town," Scarlett said. "Good luck."

Hitch gave a sharp nudge to Casey with the heels of his boots. The powerful horse bolted forward and galloped out of town, carrying Hitch toward Shadow Gap—and a showdown with the thieving Camarillo Kid.

chapter 3

The Camarillo Kid had a few hours' head start.

Hitch pushed Casey to gallop hard along the dusty trail leading out of Silver Spur. He soon hit the fork in the trail and turned onto the path that brought him to Shadow Gap. The gap was a narrow, twisting slot canyon that cut through the mountains. Towering rock walls formed a passage barely wider than Casey's haunches. Hitch slowed the horse to a trot and carefully wound his way through the snaking route. A small stream crisscrossed the trail, fed by springs deep in the mountains. Casey splashed through without hesitation.

A mile in, the canyon widened to reveal the mouth of a gold mine dug into the sheer rock wall. A hand-painted sign nailed to the top beam of a wooden frame read: GILROY'S MINE—KEEP OUT!

Lying in the dirt in front of the mine, not moving, was a man.

Gilroy.

"Doggit!" Hitch exclaimed. He leaped off Casey and ran to the old prospector. He checked for a pulse and was relieved to find one. Gently, he lifted the man's head and shook his shoulders.

"Gilroy," Hitch said sharply. "Wake up, old man."

Gilroy slowly opened his eyes and tried to focus.

"Water," he croaked.

Hitch rested him back down and ran to the stream. He grabbed a large metal plate that Gilroy used to pan for gold, and scooped up some water. He quickly brought it back to Gilroy and helped him drink. Gilroy took a swallow but coughed most of it back up. The water ran down his stringy gray beard and soaked the front of his dirty shirt.

"Enough," Gilroy growled. "You'll drown me!"

Hitch dropped the pan and helped him sit up. The leathery, old prospector looked as if he'd spent decades in this canyon, far from people and plumbing. He definitely needed a bath, but Hitch didn't point that out. The mine was Gilroy's home, and he surely didn't get enough visitors to worry about silly things like proper hygiene.

Gilroy winced in pain and rubbed his head.

"You okay, old-timer?" Hitch asked.

"No, I'm not okay!" Gilroy snarled. "Do I look okay?"

"What happened?" Hitch asked.

"A rotten kid hit me with my own shovel," Gilroy growled.

"Don't surprise me none," Hitch said.

Gilroy squinted at Hitch with curiosity. "Who are you?"

"Hitchcock's the name. I'm a marshal. Been tracking that kid for days. He's a thief, and I'm guessing if he knocked you out, he was fixing to steal something. Take a look around. See if anything's missing."

Gilroy frowned, thinking. Then his eyes lit up with a sudden realization.

"Oh, no, no, no!" he cried. He scampered to his feet and ran to a wooden box that sat at the mouth of the mine. He threw open the lid and peered inside.

"He took it!" Gilroy exclaimed. "I showed it to him, and he just took it!"

"What was it?" Hitch asked.

"Everything that mattered," Gilroy said. "I finally hit the jackpot. Took me years, but I found a golden nugget that would've set me up for life. Bigger than my fist, it was. But then this kid comes in, acting like he hasn't had a drink of water in days. I offered to help him out, and what does he do? Soon as I turn my back, he whacks me over the head and makes off with my future."

Hitch took a tired breath and said, "Yup. It's what he does. I aim to track him down and put an end to his thieving adventures."

Gilroy rubbed his sore head. "That so? You any good at it?"

"I'm the best, though you wouldn't know it from what's been happening lately."

"All I wanted was a normal place to live," Gilroy said. "I was planning on selling that golden nugget and building me a home. Now I might never get out of this canyon."

"I'll get your gold back, Gilroy. That's a promise." Hitch tipped his hat and made his way toward Casey, who patiently waited for him.

Gilroy followed. "I got to warn you: gettin' through the gap ain't easy. You've got choices to make up ahead as to which way to go. None of 'em are safe."

"That so?" Hitch climbed up onto Casey. "Any advice?"

"Sure," Gilroy said. "Turn back. That's the only safe thing to do."

"I can't do that."

"Didn't think so. All I can tell you is, be ready for anything." Gilroy picked up a small wood-handled pickax with a hammer head on one side and a curved blade on the other. He offered it to Hitch. "This might come in handy."

Hitch took the ax and fastened it to Casey's saddle. "Much obliged."

"Go get 'em, Marshal!" Gilroy exclaimed.

With a quick kick from Hitch, Casey trotted on. Hitch had tracked hundreds of outlaws, and his gut told him the Kid wasn't far ahead. After many turns and stream crossings, Hitch rounded a bend and pulled the reins to stop Casey. The canyon forked into three different trails.

The trail to the right looked to be more cave than trail. Taking it could plunge Hitch into the darkness of an underground labyrinth.

The floor of the center trail was choked with vines and branches that created a tangled carpet from wall to wall. It would be treacherous going for Casey, and there was no telling what critters might be slithering below, waiting to unload venom.

The third trail was clear on the ground, but overhead a thick canopy of branches and vines blocked the sky. Anything could be hiding up there, ready to pounce.

None of the three routes looked good. Hitch examined the ground. He found no sign of the trail the Kid had taken.

"Eeny, meeny, miny," Hitch said to himself. "Let's take miny."

He coaxed Casey into a trot, taking the left trail. They passed beneath the dense tangle of branches hanging overhead. Hitch gazed upward, fearful that something might leap down on him without warning. The canyon once again narrowed for a good half mile. It then opened to a wide, flat stretch of sand, perfect for picking up the pace.

"Giddyap!" Hitch gave Casey a nudge on the haunches.

The horse galloped a few steps, then stopped so suddenly that Hitch nearly launched out of the saddle.

"Doggit, Casey!" he exclaimed. He urged the horse on, but she wouldn't budge.

"What's gotten into you?" Hitch asked with frustration.

The answer wasn't about what had gotten into Casey—it was about what Casey had gotten into. She was buried up to her horse knees in quicksand.

The stream running back and forth had mixed with sand, and the soft surface was slowly pulling Casey deeper. And deeper. The more she struggled to lift her legs, the farther she sank into the mushy mess.

"I guess miny wasn't such a good choice," Hitch said.

He had to move fast. The longer he waited, the deeper Casey would sink. He searched around, desperate for an idea. When he looked up, he got one. The thick branches in the overhead ceiling might be his way out.

He gingerly stood on Casey's saddle.

Casey didn't like that. She tried to shake him off.

"Whoa, easy, girl. Don't go throwing me, or we'll never get out of this fix." Hitch reached down and stroked her neck. Casey relaxed. Hitch found his balance and slowly stood. He reached up, but the branches were out of his grasp.

"Steady, girl." Hitch bent his knees and jumped. He grabbed for a branch but snatched nothing but air. He crashed back down on the saddle and lost his balance. Pinwheeling his arms, he struggled against gravity but managed to stay on Casey. Barely.

"*Hoo-wee.* That was not one of my better ideas."

Casey began to panic as she sank deeper into the sand. Whatever Hitch was going to do, he had to do it fast. He grabbed the coil of rope and the pickax Gilroy had given him. He looped the rope over one shoulder and grasped the pickax in one hand.

"Now or never," he said. "One...two..."

He didn't wait till three. He bent his knees and jumped. At the same time, he thrust the pickax up overhead. He had only one shot to try to hook it on a branch. Landing back on the saddle awkwardly could be a disaster.

Yes! The ax caught a branch. Hitch hung there, his feet dangling over the saddle. There was no telling how long the branch would hold. With every bit of strength he had, he pulled himself up, struggling to lift his full weight. He raised himself a few inches, then reached his free hand up to grab onto another branch. He swayed there, hanging by the pickax and one hand.

His shoulder muscles burned, but he couldn't stop to rest. He unhooked the pickax, swung forward, and hooked it onto another branch. Once sure that branch would hold, he let go with his other hand and swung ahead again, grabbing another branch. He did the same maneuver three more times, moving hand over hand, until he cleared the patch of quicksand.

He closed his eyes, held his breath, and let go. His boots hit the dirt, and he fell onto his butt. He was safe on solid ground.

But Casey wasn't. She was still stuck in the quicksand.

"We got this, girl," Hitch called over to the horse.

He dropped the pickax and pulled the coil of rope off his shoulder. Like Rangel, Hitch was good with a lasso. He held the coil in one hand and spun the other end, creating the circle of a lariat. He flung the rope toward Casey, who stood only a few yards away. The lasso landed on the saddle. Hitch pulled, and the loop tightened around the saddle horn.

"Now, let's get you out of there. Giddyap!"

Hitch yanked on the rope. Casey whinnied nervously and pulled back. "C'mon, now, work with me!"

He tugged the rope again. Casey tried to lift her legs, but it was no use. She was stuck. Hitch refused to give up. He dug in his heels and leaned back, using his legs to pull harder.

This time Casey let the rope take her. First one front leg came free of the wet sand, then the other. The patch of quicksand wasn't very large. With one step, the golden horse found solid footing. Now she had something to stand on. While Hitch kept the rope taut, Casey pulled herself the rest of the way out.

Moments later, Casey shook like a dog after a bath. A shower of wet sand swept over Hitch as he bent, breathing hard, exhausted. Casey nuzzled him with her nose.

"You're welcome," Hitch said. "It's personal now. No one messes with such a sweet horse on my watch. I'm finding that kid."

Hitch pulled himself up and saw that he and Casey were on the wrong side of the quicksand. There was no way he'd get the horse over that dangerous patch. He took the lasso off Casey's saddle and gave her a friendly pat on her cheek.

"End of the line for us, girl," he said. "I'm much obliged to you for gettin' me this far. You go on back to Gilroy now."

He swatted the horse on the hindquarters, and with a sharp whinny, Casey galloped toward Gilroy's gold mine.

Hitch now had to get across the quicksand. He jammed the pickax into his belt, then coiled the rope. He scanned the canopy of branches overhead.

"This could work," he said to himself.

He spun the end of the rope a few times to build up momentum, then let it loose. The lasso shot toward the ceiling of vines and caught on the end of a thick branch. After a sharp tug to make sure it was a solid catch, Hitch took a deep breath and started running. He leaped forward, pulled his feet up, and swung out over the dangerous patch of sand. He kept his knees tucked to his chest. When he reached the end of the swing, he stretched his legs and landed on firm ground.

He made it!

"And that's how you do that!" He pulled the rope from the branch, coiled it, and draped it over his shoulder. "I'm coming to get you, Leonard. Or whatever you call yourself."

Hitch set off on foot, through the last leg of

Shadow Gap, desperately hoping that the quicksand hadn't slowed him down so much that the trail of the Camarillo Kid had grown cold.

chapter 4

Hitch trudged through Shadow Gap, winding his way through the narrow canyon. He was tired and growing more anxious by the second. He'd tracked and captured every cattle rustler, poker cheat, bank robber, and desperado he'd ever gone after. Until now. The Camarillo

Kid was making him look bad. Hitch was good at his job—the best—but tracking down the Camarillo Kid was turning out to be a lot more difficult than he'd expected. The boy always seemed to be one step ahead of him.

But there were innocent folks relying on him. If he didn't get back the silver ore for the town of Silver Spur, they might never get their church. If the Kid got away with Gilroy's gold nugget, the old prospector might have to spend the rest of his life digging in the mine. Hitch kept moving and hoped he'd catch a break.

Finally, after what felt like a lifetime of walking, he spotted the end of the slot canyon. Desperation Gulch was in sight. Things were starting to look up—

Until Hitch looked up.

A bright flash of light swept across the sky.

Then a deep boom shook the ground and rattled Hitch's teeth. Was it thunder and lightning? That didn't seem likely. There wasn't a cloud in the sky.

"Doggit!" Hitch realized what the light was, and it wasn't good. He raced to the end of the gap and into a circular clearing ringed by massive rock formations. He found a giant patch of scorched earth, as if a huge fire had burned there. But there were no smoking embers or burned logs.

Hitch slowly turned in a circle, searching the rocks that surrounded the clearing.

"C'mon," he said under his breath. "I know you're here somewhere."

He'd almost turned a complete 360, when he caught sight of what he was hoping to see.

It was the reflection of light off a silver surface.

"Patches," he said with a relieved sigh.

Hitch ran to a line of boulders, peeked around one end, and broke out in a big smile.

"Well, hello, Patches." Hitch had found his precious ride. He patted the saddle with affection. "I hope Leonard treated you right."

He spoke to Patches as if it were a living being. It wasn't.

Patches wasn't a horse, even though it had a typical Western saddle. The leather saddle sat atop a sleek silver vehicle that looked like a cross between a motorcycle and a small jet fighter. There were handlebars, a pointed nose, double fins to the rear, and no wheels. Painted in fancy golden script just below the saddle was PATCHES. This was Hitch's precious ride.

Hitch whirled around. The Kid was nowhere to be seen. Hitch pulled up his sleeve and entered a few commands into a wide silver band around his wrist. Then he climbed onto Patches's saddle. A series of colorful buttons blinked on the control panel between Patches's handlebars. Hitch pressed the green and blue buttons simultaneously. Patches's engine whined to life. Hitch grasped the handlebars, twisted one, and the vehicle slowly lifted straight up into the air.

Hitch hovered two feet off the ground and maneuvered the flight cycle away from the rock. He turned its nose to the center of the clearing and looked to the sky.

Another streak of light flashed overhead. Only this one didn't disappear. It became larger as it drew closer. Moments later, a silver disc-shaped ship settled to the ground on the burned area in the center of the clearing, kicking up a cloud of dust. Multicolored flashing lights ringed the edge of the flying ship. A large hatch opened. A ramp slid out and settled in the dirt. The moment it hit the ground, a young woman ran out of the craft.

"It's about time!" she shouted as she raced toward Hitch. "I knew you'd get him!"

Dale Sweet wore faded jeans, boots, a bright red flannel shirt, and a black cowboy hat that she held on to for fear it would fly off as she ran.

"Where's the little rat?" Her dark hair whipped around as she looked about expectantly.

"Gone," Hitch said.

"Gone? What do you mean, gone?" Dale cried. "You sent me the signal."

"I sent the signal for you to come and fetch me," Hitch said. "I just missed him. He took off right before I got here."

Dale's brown eyes grew wide. "A ship just came up from the ground and flew by me like a scared jackrabbit. Nearly hit me, too! Do you think that was him?"

"Yep. He ain't here," Hitch said. "And Patches is. I'm guessing this is where he stashed his ship to make his getaway. The burn marks on the ground are proof."

Hitch slowly floated on Patches toward the ramp of the silver craft as Dale walked alongside.

"I hate to say I told you so, but I was afraid something like this would happen." Dale shook her head. "We never should have split up."

"I needed you to search for Leonard from the air," Hitch explained.

"Yeah, right," Dale said, annoyed. "You wanted me out of the way. I know that. But if we'd stayed together, I could've kept watch and he'd never have stolen Patches and he'd probably be in Silver Spur wearing handcuffs right about now."

"Maybe," Hitch said. "Maybe not."

"I think that's exactly what would've happened," Dale said, challenging him.

"What's done is done," Hitch said.

"Yeah, well, it ain't all done," Dale said. "There's a storm brewing at the station. We've been called back. Now."

"Now? The Kid hasn't gotten far. If we don't follow him, the trail might go cold!" Hitch cried.

"So, what do we do?" Dale asked. "It's orders from the captain."

Hitch scratched his chin, then sighed. "We go back and get it over with as quick as possible."

"Whatever you do, don't tell anyone that Leonard stole Patches," Dale said. "We don't want to get laughed at."

"Yup, best we keep that between us," Hitch agreed.

He gunned the engine and flew Patches into the open hatch of the circular ship. Dale hurried in behind him. The ramp retracted, and the hatch sealed shut. With a roar, the silver spaceship lifted off and shot into the sky.

chapter 5

Two suns, one much larger than the other, provided heat and light for Tensor-4, a planet in a galaxy far from Earth. Hitch and Dale flew their ship out of its sunshine-baked atmosphere and into the darkness of space, where they headed straight for their home base, an orbiting space station called Alterra.

Alterra was a massive, city-sized spaceport that was home to thousands of families. They lived in soaring silver-and-white structures that glistened in the warm light shining in through Alterra's clear outer skin. Though the orbiting city was super-modern, all the men and women wore blue jeans, boots, cowboy hats, and flannel shirts. It looked as if everyone had been plucked from the Wild West of Earth and launched into orbit around this far-flung planet. But instead of riding horses, they flew flight cycles, and instead of herding cattle, they grew vegetables in hydroponic gardens.

The silver spaceship entered the massive air lock and landed among a sea of similar ships. Hitch and Dale hurried down the ship's ramp and stepped onto a moving sidewalk that whisked them away from the hangar.

"I think we're in trouble," Dale said as they zipped along.

"*We're* not in trouble," Hitch replied. "*I'm* in trouble."

"But I'm your deputy. We're a team."

"We are," said Hitch. "But whatever happened down on Tensor-4 was my doing. You've got nothing to worry about."

"Except that my partner won't let me do my job," Dale shot back.

"You're a deputy," Hitch said patiently. "And a new one at that. You've only been on the job a couple of months. You need more experience."

"Exactly! And how am I supposed to get experience if you never let me do anything? At this rate, I'll never become a full-on Sky Marshal."

"It'll happen soon enough. For now, let me take the heat, all right?"

Dale didn't continue the debate. Arguing with Hitch was about as satisfying as trying to convince water that it wasn't wet. It couldn't be done.

The moving sidewalk brought them directly to a tall silver building with a giant five-pointed star emblem hanging over the door. They entered the headquarters of the Sky Marshals and were immediately greeted by a large man whose face was red with anger.

"Get in here!" he bellowed.

It was *not* a friendly greeting.

"Good to see you, too, Mayor," Hitch said calmly.

The mayor of Alterra, Jonas Wilder, was a tall man with a large gut that strained at his belt. His jet-black suit made him look more like an undertaker than a mayor. He pointed a threatening finger at Hitch and snarled, "Don't you get sassy with me, Hitchcock."

Dale stood next to Hitch, ready to take on Wilder.

Captain Fife, the head of the Sky Marshals, hurried over. He was a mousy little man, half the size of Mayor Wilder, with buggy eyes and a constant lip twitch that made it seem like he was trying to keep from smiling. But he had nothing to smile about just then.

"Let's all take a breath here," Fife said nervously. "Remember, we're on the same team."

"You let him get away," the mayor growled at Hitch. "What kind of marshal are you, anyway?"

"The kind who knows that the more time I waste up here, the farther away that thieving brat's going to get," Hitch said.

"Uh-oh," Dale said under her breath. "Here we go."

Mayor Wilder's head turned a deep shade of red that bordered on purple. "Careful, Hitch-cock. You're talking about my son."

"I'm talking about a criminal who doesn't know right from wrong," Hitch said. "Now, why do you suppose that is?"

"Oh, this ain't good," Dale whispered.

Captain Fife felt the same way. "Maybe we should all just calm down and—"

"Are you saying I didn't raise my kid right?" the mayor shot back at Hitch.

"Just stating facts," Hitch said with a shrug. "You'd know better than I do why he turned out the way he did. I hear he's more than a little spoiled. The kind of kid who gets whatever he wants, and if he doesn't, he takes it anyway."

Hitch and the mayor glared at each other.

"Captain Fife, take his badge," the mayor said coldly. "Take both of their badges. Suspend them and send another marshal down there who knows what he's doing."

"Oh, I don't think that's necessary." Fife tried to be diplomatic. "Hitchcock is my best tracker. I'm sure that—"

"I'll decide what's necessary, Fife," the mayor said without taking his eyes off Hitch. "Unless you want me to take your badge, too."

Fife didn't have the nerve to argue. "Fine. I'll handle it."

The mayor looked away from Hitch and jabbed a finger into Fife's chest, making the smaller man flinch. "It's up to you to find my son. And bring him in, unharmed."

"That's the plan," Fife agreed.

The mayor jammed his black cowboy hat back on his head, threw one last angry look at Hitch, and said, "My son may be a thief, but from what I can tell, he's smarter than you."

The mayor's words hit Hitch like a punch in

the gut, but he didn't let on.

"Get on it," the mayor said to Fife, and stormed out.

"You can't suspend us," Dale pleaded with Fife. "We're so close to getting the Kid!"

"You heard the mayor," Fife said. "I don't have a choice. I'm sorry."

"Not your fault," Hitch said. "To be honest, it don't surprise me."

"So what happens now?" Dale asked.

"You two are on desk duty," Fife said. "Until further notice."

"No!" Dale cried. "A new team will have to start from scratch. What sense does that make?"

"And I'll need your badges."

"But...this is crazy!" Dale exclaimed.

Hitch unpinned the badge from his shirt and handed it to Fife. Dale tried to come up with another argument but realized it was useless. With a huff, she gave her badge to Fife.

"Soon as we bring in the Camarillo Kid," said Fife, "I'll be sure to—"

"Leonard," Hitch said.

"What?" Fife asked, momentarily confused.

"The mayor's son. His name's Leonard. He doesn't need a clever nickname."

"Right. As soon as we bring Leonard in, you'll get your badges back. Until then, don't leave Alterra. Better still, don't leave headquarters."

"I'll be taking the rest of the day off." Hitch strode for the door.

"Well...okay," Fife said. "Good idea. Maybe it's best you steer clear until this blows over."

Hitch left without another word.

Dale scowled at Fife. "You should've stood up for us."

Fife could only offer her a helpless shrug.

Dale followed Hitch outside. He was already on a moving sidewalk, so she had to run to catch up.

"It ain't right," she said, breathless. "This is our case. We can track that little weasel better than anybody."

She waited for a reaction. Any reaction.

She didn't get one.

"Ain't you upset?" she shouted, frustrated.

"No sense in being upset. It won't change a thing," Hitch said.

"But we can't just give up and run away with our tails between our legs!"

"Who said anything about running away?" Hitch asked. "Or givin' up?"

Dale stared at Hitch, not sure what he meant. "But Captain Fife told us to—"

Hitch gave her a little wink. Dale stopped

talking. That wasn't like him. Hitch didn't wink.

"We're still on the case, ain't we?" she said with a knowing smile.

"Not officially," Hitch said.

"*Hoo-wee!* Now we're talking! What's the plan?"

"We track him. I don't care what Mayor Wilder thinks. There hasn't been a thief born yet who can outwit me. Especially not little Leonard Wilder. But Tensor-4 is a mighty big planet. We can't just jump on a ship and head down there without any idea of what he might do next."

"He's certain to keep on stealing," Dale said. "Or maybe he'll try to sell what he already stole. He'll need grub, and you can't eat a chunk of gold. If you ask me, he's not being very smart."

"How's that?"

"Well, he stole some mighty valuable things, but they won't do him no good unless he can sell 'em. Where will he find somebody with that kind of money? I mean, a giant gold nugget? A heavy chunk of silver? A diamond the size of an apple? Those things are downright priceless."

"I agree. It don't make sense that—" Hitch stopped midsentence. "Hold on, what's this about a big diamond?"

"You didn't know? He stole a big diamond from the science museum up here on Alterra just before he took off for Silver Spur. The thing's so big and rare that it's got a name."

"Are you talkin' about the Tell Diamond?" Hitch asked.

"That's the one! Biggest diamond in the whole science museum. I saw it once. It's so big."

"That diamond is famous. I didn't know Leonard stole it."

"See?" Dale said. "That's why you need a smart

partner. If you ask me, there's no way Leonard can sell those three things."

Hitch looked worried. More worried than Dale had ever seen. He scratched his scruffy beard.

"You're thinking 'bout something. What is it?" Dale asked.

"The Trinity. We're going back to base." Hitch vaulted over the handrail of the moving sidewalk and raced in the opposite direction, toward Sky Marshal headquarters.

"Hey, wait!" Dale jumped over the rail and ran after him. "What's a Trinity?"

chapter 6

Hitch and Dale ran back to the Sky Marshal headquarters, sprinted through the lobby and into the elevator tube. The door slid closed and they shot skyward toward a higher floor.

"You want to tell me why you're so fired up about this Tell Diamond?" Dale asked. Hitch was still frowning with worry.

"Didn't cross my mind at first," he said. "Even after Leonard stole those big chunks of gold and silver. But if he took that diamond, that *particular* diamond, well, that may change everything."

"How? What's the difference?"

"Difference is between a few folks losing something valuable and a disaster that could hurt a whole lot of people. Maybe even the whole planet."

The tube door slid open and Hitch hurried out.

"That explains exactly nothing!" Dale called as she followed.

They sprinted toward a door marked LIBRARY #1. The door slid open and they entered a tiny room. A large flat-screen computer monitor took up most of one wall.

"You lookin' up something in particular?" Dale asked as the door slid shut.

"Rivindale," Hitch replied.

"Oh." She thought for a moment and added, "What's that?"

Hitch touched the clear glass and slid his finger across the surface. The screen lit up as the room lights dimmed automatically.

"Show me the map of Tensor-4," Hitch commanded the screen.

A huge photographic map of the planet appeared on the screen.

"There are over three hundred different colonies of people on Tensor-4," Hitch explained. "Most of these groups came from other planets. Each brought their own way of life and history here. There's the cat-people of Eelong, the invisible clans of Wells, and the giants of Prox."

"And us," Dale said. "From Alterra."

"Right," Hitch said. "It's our job to keep the peace between all the different colonies."

As he spoke, Hitch swiped his hand across the glass, moving the image of the map this way and that, zooming in and zooming out, searching the planet.

"They all came to Tensor-4 for the same reason, to start a new life in a place where nobody judges you for not being the same as them."

"Tell me something I don't know," Dale said.

"Rivindale," Hitch said. "A colony I'm having trouble finding right about now."

He continued to swipe through the map, hunting through aerial views of the terrain of Tensor-4.

"Never heard of it," Dale said.

"Just as well. Their home planet of Rivin is a beautiful place. The Rivins are peaceful, but except for one clan. They thought of themselves as royalty and felt they should be ruling the entire planet."

"I'm guessing nobody else agreed with them," Dale said.

"You guessed right. But this clan of rebels was a powerful group. They were smart and rich. They had all sorts of resources and built themselves an army."

"You mean they built weapons?" Dale asked.

"No, they built a whole army. These rebels made mechanical men. Fighting robots with no fear. Dozens of 'em. The rebels sent them to march on the capital to overthrow the rightful government, but the Rivin army was bigger. And stronger. They defeated the mechanical army and destroyed it, and the rebels were kicked off the planet."

"They got thrown off their own planet?" Dale asked.

"Yup."

"Let me guess. They ended up on Tensor-4?"

"Yup again. They started a colony called Rivindale."

An overhead view of a medieval castle built on top of a wooded hill surrounded by a village of thatch-roofed huts appeared on the screen.

"Looks like something out of a kid's fairy tale." Dale whistled in awe.

"Except it's not. The Sky Marshals have been keeping an eye on the rebels to make sure they don't try anything nasty like they did on Rivin. That's how I know about 'em"

"So what is this Trinity thing?" Dale asked.

"I don't know, exactly. But from what I hear, it's a weapon the rebels used when they tried to conquer their home planet. This bunch isn't just evil, they're smart. Brilliant, maybe. They figured out a way to transform natural metals into a powerful weapon."

"Gold and silver?" Dale asked. "Those aren't weapons."

"Not normally, but it's all about the Tell Diamond. It's not found anywhere else in the universe except on Rivin."

"The diamond Leonard stole is from Rivin? What's it doing in a museum here?"

"You'd have to ask Mayor Wilder. He's the one who brought it here. That diamond has some kind of special properties. From what I hear, when it comes in contact with gold and silver, a chemical reaction takes place that transforms the metals into something powerful. Something dangerous. It's evil alchemy. I'm not entirely sure what this power can do, but for certain it causes destruction, because that's what happened on Rivin. A whole city was leveled before the Rivin army put the rebels out of business."

"And Leonard stole the three elements that make up the Trinity," said Dale. "Do you think he's planning on giving 'em to the Rivins?"

Hitch nodded. "If the Rivins get their diamond back, along with those big chunks of gold and silver, they could have a mighty strong weapon."

"So they could conquer Tensor-4 and destroy us all?"

Hitch nodded again. "I sure do hope I'm wrong."

Hitch lifted his sleeve and inputted the information running across the bottom of the screen onto his silver Sky Marshal computer wristband. Then he swiped his hand across the screen. The image of the castle disappeared, and the room lights came back up.

"Something doesn't sit right with me," Dale said. "I don't get how Leonard was able to steal the Tell Diamond from the museum. He's a kid, not some master criminal."

"Good question. I guess when your father's the mayor, you get into places you shouldn't," Hitch said. "But however he got it, if Leonard's got the Tell Diamond, he's got the Trinity. He could be on his way to Rivindale with it right now."

"To help 'em start a war," Dale said, horrified. "Do you know how to get there?"

Hitch tapped the computer band on his arm. "I do now. It's why we came back here."

"So let's get going!" Dale started for the door but stopped suddenly. "Wait. Is the Trinity something everybody knows about?"

"Nope," Hitch replied. "It's top secret. The only mention of it is in the secure Sky Marshal database."

Dale turned back to the screen and called out,

"Show us the last person who searched for the Trinity, the Tell Diamond, and the Rivins."

The room grew dark, and an image appeared on the screen. Dale and Hitch both gasped. It was a picture of Leonard Wilder—the Camarillo Kid—searching through the computer's database.

"I guess that proves it," Dale said. "He really does get in places he shouldn't be."

"Yup," Hitch said. "Let's go get him."

chapter 7

Hitch and Dale walked faster than the moving sidewalk, dodging around the people standing still. When they reached the hangar where the flying ships were parked, Hitch turned to Dale. "I'm getting second thoughts about this."

"Why? You saw the picture. Leonard knows

about the Trinity for sure!"

"That's not what I mean. Going off like this could get you in big trouble with Captain Fife. Not to mention Mayor Wilder. It could hurt your chances of becoming a full Sky Marshal. I don't think you should come along."

The idea made Dale stop and think for a moment, but no more than that. "Too late." She tried to push past Hitch, but he stopped her.

"No, it ain't. Take the day off."

"I don't want the day off," Dale said. "I'm going with my partner."

"That's right professional of you, but you know I work best alone."

"I don't know any such thing," Dale said. "You think you do, but you're dead wrong."

"I ain't wrong. Go home." He started toward the hangar, but Dale jumped in front of him.

"You listen to me, William Hitchcock. You may think you got it all covered, but you don't. Not all the time, anyway. Everybody needs somebody to watch their back. Maybe you more than most 'cause you're always going places where you shouldn't be going and getting in scrapes you shouldn't be in. I'm your partner. So, either I go with you, or I blow the whistle and make sure this ship never leaves the station. At least not with you on it. Don't think that I won't do it, 'cause I will."

Hitch stared at Dale. "Would you, really?"

Dale softened. "No, I wouldn't, but we are going together whether you like it or not."

Hitch was about to keep arguing but realized it was useless. He saw nothing but stubborn in her fiery eyes. "Suit yourself," he said.

Dale silently pumped her fist in victory.

The two entered the hangar, threw a couple of casual waves to the ground crew, who had no idea the two were suspended and not supposed to be there, and boarded their ship. Moments later, the ramp retracted and the hatch sealed. With a powerful roar, the silver ship lifted off the deck and streaked across Alterra, headed for the air lock. In minutes, they were back in open space and orbiting Tensor-4.

Together, they worked the controls. Hitch's eyes locked on the navigation screen, checking it against the coordinates of Rivindale on his computer band, while Dale piloted the ship.

Dale watched Hitch for a long moment. She'd been his partner for nearly half a year and had yet to figure out exactly what made him tick.

"I need you to be honest with me," she said quietly.

"I don't lie," Hitch said.

"Good, then don't start now. Am I that bad of a deputy?"

Hitch gave her a quick look, as if surprised by the question. "I got no complaints."

"Then why won't you let me help you? Like, ever? I know you say I'm still new, but I've been at this awhile now. It's got to be something else."

Hitch gave the question some serious thought before answering.

"It ain't you," he finally said. "It's just what I'm used to. Ma passed before I was old enough to remember, so it was always just me and Pa. He didn't want much to do with raisin' a young 'un, so I pretty much had to take care of myself. I guess I got used to doing things on my own, is all."

"Is that why you don't like Mayor Wilder?"

Dale asked. "Seeing as how his kid turned out?"

"There are a lot of reasons I don't like that windbag, but I can't say it's the mayor's fault that he's got a weasel for a son. Leonard needs to be responsible for himself. But from what I can see, his pa didn't do much to teach the kid right from wrong. Who knows? If he had, maybe we wouldn't be out here tracking him down."

"You might be right," Dale said. "Look, I'm not saying you should change who you are or how you feel, but there's no shame in taking a little help sometimes."

"I'll try to remember that." Hitch focused back on the navigation screen.

Dale didn't believe him for a second. But it was no use trying to force the issue. Hitch was too stubborn. She gazed out the ship's forward window at the blue-green planet below.

"It surely is a remarkable world we've got here," she said.

"You get no argument from me," Hitch said. "Where else are you going to find hundreds of different kinds of people who started off on different planets and came to a new world to live side by side?"

"Peacefully," Dale added.

"Yeah, peacefully," Hitch echoed. "Let's make sure it stays that way."

With that, Dale fired the retro rockets, and their ship dropped down into the atmosphere of Tensor-4, headed for the mysterious town of Rivindale.

"We're in luck," Hitch said. "Nighttime. We have a chance to poke around without being seen."

They descended through a thick layer of clouds. Though it was dark, they could easily make out the massive castle they'd seen on the computer screen. It had multiple pointed towers on each of the four corners of the central open-air courtyard.

"That sure is one fancy shack. For people banished from their home, they got it pretty good," Dale said.

"Must be how folks live in Rivin," Hitch said. "Everybody tries to bring a little piece of home to Tensor-4 with them. I guess the Rivin rebels are no different."

"Why is it so dark?" Dale asked. "Ain't nobody home?"

"Don't know," Hitch replied. "Maybe they turn in early in these parts."

A tall, imposing stone wall ringed the castle. The only way in was through giant wooden doors.

Dale circled the ship high above the castle, looking for a safe place to land. She found a grassy meadow on the far side of the hill. The only sign of life was a herd of grazing sheep. Dale maneuvered the ship and gently landed near a stand of leafy trees.

"So far so good," Dale said. "What's the plan?"

"I'll fly to the castle on Patches. Have a look around," Hitch said. "You stay here and protect the ship in case we're spotted."

"What? No! Didn't you hear anything I said? I'm going *with* you!"

"I heard, but you need to stay here. We don't want any Rivins getting hold of this ship. They'll steal it, for sure. If they show up, you take off right quick."

"But—"

"That's final, Deputy," Hitch said with

authority. "This time I ain't givin' in."

Dale wanted to argue. She wanted to go with Hitch. She wanted to do her job and, if she was being totally honest, she wanted some excitement. It's why she joined the Sky Marshals. It wasn't enough to offer Hitch ideas and advice. She'd done that plenty of times. And plenty of times it got him out of some serious scrapes, not that Hitch would've admitted it. Dale wanted in on the action. Sitting on her hands doing nothing wasn't cutting it anymore.

But as much as she hated to admit it, she also understood how important it was to protect the ship.

"In time, you'll get plenty of chances to jump into it," Hitch said, as if he'd read her mind.

"Yeah, right," Dale said sarcastically. "Be honest. It's mostly because you work alone."

"That's part of it, too."

"Then maybe it's time I started lookin' for a new partner." Dale plopped down in the pilot's seat of the ship, folded her arms, and stared out the window.

Hitch was torn. He wanted to square things with Dale, but he was racing the clock to stop a potential planet-wide disaster.

"Let's sort this out after we finish the mission," Hitch said. "I'll be back before you know it. Hopefully with Leonard in cuffs."

Dale didn't respond. She was angry, and she wanted him to know it.

Hitch climbed aboard Patches and checked his gear. He still had the lasso from Rangel and the pickax from Gilroy. He took a last glance at Dale, then rose into the air and flew through the hatch and out of the ship.

Dale didn't turn to watch him go.

The dark night was the perfect cover. Hitch flew Patches toward the castle, close to the ground until he reached the trees just short of the towering wall. After a quick look around to make sure he hadn't been seen, he gunned the flight cycle and rose straight up, flew over the top of the wall, then quickly dropped to the ground on the other side. He waited. No alarms. Nobody came running. He was in.

The clouds had cleared. Since no lights burned inside the castle, Hitch could only see by the scant light from the nighttime stars. He didn't mind. It meant less chance of getting caught.

He left Patches and continued on foot. With the coil of rope around his shoulder and the pickax in his belt, Hitch sprinted across the grass and entered the castle. He found himself in a grand hall with a soaring ceiling and a wide staircase.

At the bottom of the stairs stood two medieval-looking knights in silver armor. They stood at attention, their faces covered by silver helmets. Each guard held a long spear.

"Doggit!" Hitch whispered.

His secret arrival wouldn't be a secret for long. He'd have to fight his way past these two guards.

Back on the ship, Dale drummed her fingers on the arm of the pilot's chair. She grew angrier by the minute. This wasn't why she'd joined the Sky Marshals. She'd done all the training, passed every test, and proved that she was as smart and resourceful as any of the other deputies. The last thing she'd expected was to be sitting by herself while her partner did all the work.

It wasn't only about her ego. If the Rivin rebels got hold of the Trinity, there'd be serious trouble on Tensor-4. Maybe even a war. People could get hurt. It was frustrating to be left behind when there was so much at stake.

Dale made a decision. She was going after Hitch. She jumped to her feet and headed for the hatch. Then her eye caught movement outside. She froze. Was it a tree branch blowing around? Leaves kicked up by the wind? Or was somebody out there?

She and Hitch had landed in a colony filled with rebels who'd tried to conquer their home world. The Rivins had failed and were sent to Tensor-4. They didn't want to be here, and Dale was in a spaceship that could get them out. Perhaps protecting the ship was pretty important after all.

She turned out every light on the ship, throwing herself into darkness. Cautiously stepping forward, she moved closer to the front window to get a better look outside. She hoped to see a stray sheep or a tumbleweed blowing by.

A face appeared through the window directly in front of her.

Then another.

And a third. All bald men wearing black. It was so dark outside there was no way to tell how many there were.

Dale yelped and jumped backward, nearly falling over the pilot's seat.

Outside, the man in the center smiled.

The Rivin rebels had arrived.

chapter 8

At the castle, Hitch was outnumbered two to one.

He grabbed the lasso from his shoulder, holding the loop in one hand. If he used the rope to trip up the knights, he could sprint past them and up the stairs. But he'd have to find Leonard fast.

The Rivins would not take kindly to a stranger running through their castle.

Hitch sprinted across the hall, ready to whip the rope at whichever knight moved first. He drew close, but neither moved. Hitch's hopes grew. It was going to be a total surprise! He was nearly on them, and still, neither so much as turned their head to look his way. Hitch cocked his arm, ready to fling the rope, but the knights still didn't react.

Huh? He stopped running and stood a few feet from them, waiting for either to move.

Neither did. Hitch approached one cautiously. He walked right up to him. Still nothing. He tentatively reached out and poked the knight's chest with his finger. No reaction.

"What's your story, pardner?" Hitch said. "Are you a scarecrow?"

Hitch spotted a round knob attached to a small door built into the armor. He reached for it and pulled the door open.

"Well, I'll be!" he exclaimed at the complex series of gears and cogs inside the knight's chest. This guard was more clock than man.

"They're up to their old tricks," he said. The mechanical man was proof that he was right about the Rivins. They were building an army of robots on Tensor-4.

Hitch's heart raced. He was sure Leonard was in the castle and had brought the Trinity. His mission had become more important than ever.

The Kid had to be stopped.

Hitch moved past the two frozen robots and ran up the grand staircase, taking two steps at a time. On the second level, he entered a wide corridor lined with ornate tapestries—and more robots.

Two rows of knights stood shoulder-to-shoulder, facing each other. Hitch's stomach twisted. The Rivins had created dozens of robots! How had they managed to build these complex machines while the Sky Marshals were supposedly keeping an eye on them? Hitch shook away the thought. He had more pressing problems to worry about.

These robots were also inactive, but Hitch walked past them cautiously, fearing they might spring to life at any moment. As he moved, he searched the corridors on either side, hoping to spot Leonard.

He hit another staircase and bounded up. Two more knights stood at the top. Like the robots below, they were no more of a threat than statues in a museum. At least for now. He ran down this corridor, scanning left and right. At the end, he rounded a corner and came upon an archway leading to the wide open-air courtyard they'd seen from the air.

In the center of the courtyard was a large marble throne.

Sitting on the throne was a woman.

And she moved.

She was no statue! As soon as she locked eyes with Hitch, she stood.

Now we're getting somewhere, Hitch thought. He ran into the courtyard.

He'd only gone a few steps when he jolted back. It felt as if someone were grabbing him. But no one was there.

"Wha—?" Hitch gasped with confusion.

He fought to move his arms and legs, but he was held tight. Hitch looked around, desperate to understand what was happening. A spotlight

perched on a tower high above sprang to life—
and he suddenly understood the fix he was in.

The light reflected off a giant spiderweb. The
ropelike webbing stretched from one end of the
courtyard to the other and reached three stories
above him. The web was coated in a sticky sub-
stance, and he couldn't pull away from its grip.
He was stuck…and then he heard a mechanical
sound.

A spider crawled out from a dark alcove.

A mechanical spider.

A *huge* mechanical spider. It was five feet long
with eight metal legs and sharp pincers that
looked big enough and powerful enough to cut a
man in half.

And it was headed toward Hitch.

Back on the ship, Dale hit the control that closed

the hatch. She started to press the communicator to contact Hitch, then stopped. Was it the right thing to do? Hitch was trying to sneak into the castle, unnoticed. Her voice blasting from the band on his wrist would give him away for sure. No, that would be a mistake.

Clang! Clang! Clang!

It sounded as though the Rivins were pounding on the hull with hammers. Were they trying to break in? What were Hitch's instructions? If the Rivins showed up, she was supposed to take off. They couldn't get hold of the ship. That was her mission. She jumped into the pilot's seat and began the process of powering up.

"Greetings," called an eerie, muffled voice from outside.

Three Rivins stood in front of the ship. They wore all black, which made their bald heads appear to float in space, lit only by starlight.

"A word of warning," the Rivin in the middle said calmly. "We've attached powerful mines to your ship. If you take off, as soon as you gain altitude and the pressure changes, they will explode. Your ship will be destroyed, and you along with it. My advice is to open the hatch and come out. We wouldn't want you to get hurt."

Dale froze. Was he telling the truth? Were the clanging noises the sounds of them attaching explosives to the hull? Or was he bluffing to get her to come out so they could steal the ship?

The excitement that Dale was looking for had finally arrived.

And she had no idea what to do.

The monster mechanical spider crept slowly toward Hitch. Its hairy legs moved easily across the sticky web. Hitch struggled to reach the pickax tucked into his belt, but the gooey web held him back.

"For a smart marshal, you sure are easy to fool." A voice came from the shadows of the courtyard.

Hitch's stomach fell. He knew that voice. Any hope that he'd been wrong about the Trinity and the Rivins was gone.

The Camarillo Kid stepped out from behind one of the many pillars that ringed the courtyard. The fourteen-year-old boy who'd run into the Mine Car Hotel, desperately looking for help, was no more. Now he stood tall with his hands on his hips, his white cowboy hat tipped back casually, and a smug smile on his face.

"Evenin', Leonard," Hitch said casually. He made sure to show no sign that he was surprised or upset by his own impending doom.

The Kid's smile dropped. "I ain't Leonard no more."

"Aww, you'll always be Little Leonard to me."

The Kid looked as though he'd erupt with anger, but he stayed in control and his conceited smile returned. "Maybe so, but it don't matter. Pretty soon I won't be the Camarillo Kid, either. I'm getting a new title. Sir Camarillo, Captain of the Guard."

"Is that so? How'd you get such a fancy title?" Hitch asked while keeping an eye on the monster spider. It had stopped moving.

"I joined up with the Rivins," the Kid said proudly. "Lady Tell's putting me in charge of a whole regiment of knights. We're going to march all over this planet, and I'm getting me my own town to run. Think I'll call it Camarillo City. Has a nice ring to it, don't you think?"

"And who might Lady Tell be?" Hitch asked.

"That would be me." A woman stepped out of the shadows behind the Kid.

Lady Tell was the woman Hitch had seen on the throne. She was dressed in a black leather cloak with silver trim, looking every bit the warrior-queen. She had black hair that fell to her waist and a small silver tiara. Her intense, emotionless gaze fell on Hitch, as if she, too, were a spider sizing up its prey.

"You've entered my home without an invitation," Lady Tell said coldly. "For that alone I should let my pet devour you."

Hitch tried not to look at the spider that rested only a few feet away.

"My apologies," Hitch said. "Just lookin' for the boy here. He's been a might naughty."

"Ha!" The Kid laughed. "Naughty? That what

you call it? I pulled off three impossible robberies, then took your flight cycle and all your gear. I am way past naughty."

"Can't argue with you there, Leonard," Hitch said.

"The Camarillo Kid has been very helpful to me," Lady Tell said. "He should be rewarded."

"See?" the Kid said with a smirk. "And stop callin' me Leonard."

Hitch ignored him and focused on the woman. "Lady Tell? Like the Tell Diamond?"

The woman offered a small smile. "You know of it?"

"A little," Hitch replied. "I know it's a special diamond that turns gold and silver into something powerful. You used that power to make trouble on your home planet. But it didn't work out and you got sent here to this prison."

"You think Rivindale is a prison?" She waved her arm around as if showing off the majestic castle. "Does this look like a prison to you?"

"Don't matter how fancy a place is. If you can't leave, it's a prison."

"Then you don't know anything at all," Lady Tell said with an evil smile that made the hair on the back of Hitch's neck go up.

"What we started on Rivin we'll finish here on Tensor-4," she said. "Our clan has the means to overrun every last one of the colonies on this strange little planet. We'll unite them under one banner—ours—and then turn our attention to the sky and Alterra. We will rule this planet and then return to Rivin and stake our rightful claim."

Hitch whistled. "That's some seriously strange plan you got going on there."

"You doubt our abilities?" Lady Tell asked.

"Can't speak to that one way or the other," Hitch said. "But there's something I don't get. How did you build all the robot knights I saw downstairs? Especially when the Sky Marshals were keeping watch?"

"I believe I can answer that." Mayor Wilder stepped out of the shadows. "The Rivins have a friend on Alterra."

chapter 9

"Come out, come out," the bald Rivin called to Dale in a singsong voice. "You don't want us to blow open the hatch, now, do you?"

Dale's mind raced. She was scared. *Really* scared.

"What do you want from me?" she called out.

"From you? Nothing at all," the Rivin called back. "You're free to go. We want your ship."

Hitch was right. They wanted the ship. Did they plan to use it to escape from Tensor-4? Or was it for something worse? If Leonard had brought them the Trinity, there was no telling what kind of mayhem they could spread across Tensor-4 with a flying ship.

No, they couldn't get the ship. It would be better if it was destroyed.

And Dale knew how.

"Okay!" Dale called. "I'm coming out."

She had to work fast. If the Rivins suspected that something wasn't right, they might blow up the ship. "Just getting my gear together," Dale yelled.

Dale had no gear. But she had a checklist in her head. She'd memorized it at the Sky Marshal

Academy. All deputies were taught to be prepared for situations like this one. It was a drastic move, but Dale saw no other way. She stood over the cockpit controls and entered a series of special commands.

"We're waiting!" the Rivin called out.

Her fingers flew over the control console, inputting the commands in what she hoped was the exact right order because she wouldn't be getting a second chance. There were twenty commands in all. When she reached the final one, she held her breath and threw the last toggle switch.

Instantly, every light on the cockpit panel flashed red.

"Yes!" Dale pumped her fist in victory.

She'd done it. The ship was disabled. Forever. No command could make it ever fly again. From that moment on, the ship was about as useful as a garbage dumpster.

"Time's up!" The Rivin was losing his patience.

"Okay, I'm coming out!" Dale ran to the far side of the ship, where her flight cycle, LuluBelle, sat. She jumped into the saddle and powered up. LuluBelle rose a few inches off the deck. Dale punched a command into her wristband computer, and the ship's hatch door began to rise.

She gunned LuluBelle's engine and sped forward. The door had barely risen halfway, but Dale couldn't wait for it to open all the way. Those last few seconds could mean the difference between getting caught and escaping. Dale ducked her head. Her shoulder grazed the bottom of the rising door, nearly knocking her off LuluBelle. She flew through the opening with barely an inch to spare overhead.

Dale shot away from the ship, past the group of surprised Rivins, and into the night.

At the castle, Mayor Wilder strolled up to Hitch with his hands in his pockets and a smile on his face.

"I got to hand it to you, Hitchcock." He shook his head with dismay. "I didn't kick you off this case because you couldn't track down Leonard. I wanted you gone because I thought you *would*. And sure enough, here you are."

"Pa!" the Kid cried. "Stop calling me Leonard!"

"Sorry, son. I meant to say, Sir Camarillo."

"That's better." The Kid gave him a big, satisfied grin.

It was clear to Hitch that Leonard was used to getting his way, even from his tough father.

"Let me get this straight," Hitch said to the

mayor. "You're friends with these here Rivins?"

"More than just friends," he replied. "I guess you could call us partners."

"But why?" Hitch asked.

"I'm tired, Hitchcock. Tired of floating around in that space station, riding herd over a bunch of do-gooders like you who do nothing but solve problems for the people of Tensor-4, and they don't even appreciate it. I want a piece of the action down here for myself."

"Me too," the Kid said. "It's boring up on Alterra."

"So you joined up with a bunch of desperados?" Hitch asked.

"I wouldn't say that. I'm the one who brought the rebels here. I saw a chance to use their power to claim a piece of Tensor-4 for myself and my boy." He put his arm around Leonard's shoulder.

"That explains a lot," Hitch said. "I suppose you gave 'em everything they needed to build all those robots."

The mayor raised both of his hands, palms up, and said, "Guilty."

The pieces were falling together and Hitch didn't like how the puzzle was turning out.

"It took 'em a while, but we're just about ready to get started," the mayor said.

"Doing what?" Hitch asked.

Lady Tell stepped forward. "First we'll attack and conquer the small clans close to us. Then we'll march across Tensor-4, eating up colonies one by one to create a single, massive kingdom."

"With Lady Tell as their queen," the mayor added.

"And I'll get to be boss of my own town," the Kid said. "Maybe two towns!"

"What about you?" Hitch asked the mayor. "What do you get?"

Wilder smiled broadly. "I'll rule alongside Lady Tell. We'll be partners."

"And the peaceful people in all the colonies have no say in it?" Hitch said.

"Not unless they want to be crushed by the Rivin army," Lady Tell answered.

Hitch let it all sink in. "What kind of father gets his kid involved in such a nasty plan?"

The mayor and Leonard both burst out laughing.

"I did nothing of the sort," the mayor said.

"It wasn't Pa's idea at all. I came up with the whole thing!" the Kid said with a proud smile.

"It's true," the mayor added. "He's the one who thought to bring the Rivins here. It was his idea to help 'em build an army to conquer Tensor-4.

He's the one who tracked down the pieces of the Trinity. This all came from him."

"Makes me kind of sad," Hitch said. "You may not have done anything to turn the kid mean, but you sure didn't do much to stop it from happening, either."

"And that's just fine by me because one day, I'll be king of Tensor-4," the Kid said.

"I think the people of Tensor-4 might have a little something to say about that," Hitch said defiantly.

"Then you don't understand the power of the Trinity." Lady Tell turned and strode back across the courtyard, headed for her throne.

"She means business," the Kid said with a chuckle. "You're gonna wish that spider got to you first."

Hitch threw a quick glance to the quiet spider,

hoping it would stay quiet. Then he watched Lady Tell.

Next to her throne sat a glass tank the size of a refrigerator filled with red liquid. Thick cables ran from the bottom of the clear tank to three tall metal towers. On top of each tower was a metal propeller. Lady Tell reached into a small wooden box and pulled out the rough Tell Diamond from Rivin, the silver ore from the town of Silver Spur, and the gold nugget from Gilroy's mine.

The Trinity.

"The robots are just piles of gears and springs without power," the Kid explained. "That's what the Trinity gives 'em. Power."

Lady Tell placed the diamond, silver, and gold on pedestals on top of the clear tank. A glass dome lowered over them. She flipped a switch and a flame ignited beneath. Quickly, the water in the tank heated up and began to boil. Dark red steam rose into the glass dome that held the three elements. Within moments, thick red steam filled the dome so completely that the elements couldn't be seen.

"You're about to witness something quite spectacular," Lady Tell told Hitch.

She flipped another switch, and a white laser beam cut through the red steam. It hit the diamond, lighting it up so brightly that Hitch had to squint. The glowing gem floated in the sea of red, growing brighter by the second.

A moment later, the laser light passed through the diamond and split in two, sending out two red lasers, which hit the gold and the silver, making both chunks of metal glow nearly as bright as the diamond.

Lady Tell gazed at the glowing metals with

pride. "Light that passes through the Tell Diamond energizes the two metals and stitches them together to create something wonderful."

The metal propellers on the top of the three towers began to spin, powered by the Trinity's magical energy. The blades picked up speed, spinning faster and faster. Each gave off a steady hum. At that exact moment, millions of tiny white lights sparked to life, turning night into day. The castle lit up like an amusement park attraction.

"This is the power of the Trinity." Lady Tell turned to the Kid. "Thank you. The metals you brought me are pure and perfect."

"It's a right impressive trick," Hitch said. "But I'm not seeing the point."

Lady Tell laughed. "Oh, you will."

A robot knight standing silently in the shadows suddenly jolted to life. Light glowed from the seams in its armor. The knight lifted its spear and held it point out, ready for battle.

"The energy created by the Trinity travels through the air in waves," Lady Tell said. "The power it carries is limitless."

Hitch's mouth went dry. He tried to swallow but couldn't. "So all those knights I passed down below...?"

"They're about to wake up," Lady Tell replied.

Deep down in the halls of the castle, the dozens of knights that had been standing shoulder-to-shoulder tensed up as the invisible wave of energy hit them. The glow from the power of the Trinity seeped out of every seam in their armor, giving them an eerie radiance. They moved their arms forward and back as if trying out their new-found abilities. Each had a spear. Each was ready to use it.

The Rivins' army had come to life.

And the spider had powered back up. It's eyes flashed red as the wave of energy from the whirling towers washed over it. Once again, it was on the move—toward Hitch.

"Cut me loose, Leonard," Hitch said. "You ain't a killer."

"Don't listen to him," the mayor scolded. "This is all part of the plan."

The Kid watched the spider inch ever closer to Hitch. Its powerful pincers were open, ready to clamp down on its helpless victim.

For the first time, the Kid looked unsure. "I think maybe we scared him enough," he told Lady Tell. "You can call off your spider."

"Why would you say that? This man has been hunting you down. Wouldn't you like to see him snapped in two?"

"Uh, not really," he said. "I just wanted to scare him a little. I don't want him getting hurt."

Lady Tell laughed. "What do you think is going to happen once we attack the colonies? This isn't a game. People will get hurt. Some will die."

The Kid turned to his father. "You said everybody'd fall into line, once they saw they didn't have a chance."

"I'm sure some will," he said with a shrug. "But not all. This is war, son."

"I...I'm not so sure that's a good thing," the Kid said.

"Leonard!" Hitch yelled. "I mean, Camarillo. Be brave. Do the right thing. Stop this."

The Kid backed away from Hitch. He truly didn't know what to do.

A steady *thump, thump, thump* echoed around them.

"What's that sound?" the Kid asked.

"My army is making its way here," Lady Tell said.

The pounding footsteps of the marching knights grew louder as their metal feet hammered against the stone stairs, climbing ever closer.

"You should feel honored, Hitchcock," Mayor Wilder called. "You're about to go down in history as the first victim of the new order."

"Lucky me." Hitch's eyes never left the monster spider.

"That's not entirely true," Lady Tell said. "He won't be the first victim."

A glowing knight suddenly appeared and lunged forward, pointing his spear directly at the mayor's chest.

"Whoa, now!" the mayor exclaimed. "What's all this?"

"It's the end of your story," Lady Tell said. "I want to thank you and Leonard for all you did for us. Now that we have the Trinity, we won't be needing you any longer."

"No! No!" The mayor shook his head angrily. "That wasn't our deal. We're partners. I'm going to be king!"

"Well...I think not," Lady Tell said. "I prefer to work alone."

"But you owe everything to me!" The mayor's face turned dark red with rage.

"I suppose we do," Lady Tell said. "Unfortunately there's one thing you didn't understand. You can never trust a villain."

She nodded to the knight, who thrust his spear at the mayor. The mayor dodged out of the way, then tripped and landed on his butt.

The Kid reached down and quickly helped

his father to his feet as the knight advanced. The Kid and the mayor backed away until they hit a stone wall.

Trapped.

"Do something, Pa," he cried.

"Lady Tell! Stop this!" the mayor shouted.

She didn't.

Hitch desperately tried to break free of the web. The spider had wrapped its enormous pincers around his waist. Hitch sucked in his breath, ready for the worst.

"Eeee-haa!"

All eyes shot skyward as LuluBelle swooped over the wall with Dale in the saddle.

"Doggit!" Hitch cried with relief.

With one hand on the handlebars, Dale used the other to unfurl her special-issue Sky Marshal laser lasso. She swept the flight cycle down low and, like a rodeo cowboy roping a steer, she flung the crackling laser lasso. A lariat of light glowed brilliantly against the night sky. The lasso snagged the top of the spiderweb. Dale quickly tied the other end to the horn of her saddle, then gunned the powerful engine. The web ripped away from the castle walls and dangled from the end of her glowing lasso. Dale dragged it toward the sky with Hitch still stuck to it. The spider, now hanging below Hitch, was along for the ride as well.

Mayor Wilder grabbed his son and pulled him away from the knight. They ran through the archway that led inside the castle, but dozens of glowing knights blocked their escape. They had no choice but to run back into the courtyard.

Dangling high above the ground, the spider wouldn't give up. It climbed toward Hitch with its pincers snapping. Hitch yanked one leg free from the sticky web and kicked frantically at the mechanical beast.

"I'll bash it against the tower!" Dale called down to Hitch. "Hang on!"

"Just don't go bashing me!" Hitch called back.

Dale flew past one of the pointed spires of the castle. Her aim was perfect. The spider smashed into the tower and let out a horrifying screech. Its pincers cut wildly, slicing up the web. The spider ripped away from the sticky web and fell...

But so did Hitch.

Thinking fast, he grabbed the pickax from his belt, spun around, and snagged the ropelike web with the pick just before he dropped below its lowest point.

The spider plummeted to the ground, doomed.

With one last screech, it smashed to bits on the courtyard's stone floor.

A second more and Hitch would have met the same fate. He dangled from the shredded web, hanging on by only the small curved blade of the ax.

"Fly me down!" Hitch called out.

Dale quickly flew LuluBelle down until Hitch was only a few feet from the ground. He yanked the pickax free from the web and fell the last few feet to land safely and ready to fight.

Lady Tell leaped off her throne. Things were no longer going as she'd planned.

"Stop him!" she screamed.

The knight charged for Hitch with its spear ready.

Hitch used the pickax to defend himself, knocking the spear away again and again as the knight attacked relentlessly.

"Look!" Leonard shouted, pointing to the archway.

The army of glowing knights had arrived. In moments, they'd completely outnumber the Sky Marshals.

"There's a whole mess of these guys coming out!" Hitch called up to Dale.

"I'm on it!" Dale called back.

She flew down. The sticky spiderweb and the laser lasso still dangled below LuluBelle. As soon as the first knights marched into the courtyard, Dale dragged the web over them, tangling them up. Then she wrapped the laser lasso around them. More knights kept coming, mindlessly pushing from behind. Soon the knights were jumbled up in a sticky mess of arms, legs, laser lasso, spears, and web.

Dale had choked off their access to the court-yard!

But her flight cycle was still attached to the web by the laser lasso. She frantically tried to unhitch it from the handlebars, but it was pulled too tight. If she didn't land soon, she'd crash!

Hitch battled, but he was no match for the robot knight. Mechanical men didn't grow tired, and Hitch was losing strength, fast. With a final sweep of its spear, the knight knocked the pickax from Hitch's grasp. The tool flew across the courtyard and clattered to the stone floor, out of Hitch's reach.

Back inside the castle, the knights that weren't caught in the web backed off and circled around, heading for the side entrances to the courtyard.

The knight attacking Hitch pressed his spear directly against his chest.

"I didn't want it to be like this, Hitch," the Kid called from the corner where he was huddled with his father.

Hitch's back hit a stone column. Dead end.

Lady Tell walked up behind the knight. "Seems the mayor was right. You will be my first victim after all."

"Don't count on that!" Dale now stood in the center of the courtyard, holding the pickax.

"Break the glass!" Hitch called to her. "It's their power!"

"Stop her!" Lady Tell screamed at the knight.

The knight left Hitch and ran after Dale, its metal feet clanking across the stone floor.

All around them, the rest of the robot knights swarmed into the courtyard.

Dale sprinted for the device that was pumping out their energy.

"*Eeee-haa!*" she screamed as she flung the pickax.

The blade spun through the air and hit the glass dome, shattering it. The red steam pent up inside rose into the air and floated away. The chunks of glowing gold and silver were knocked off their pedestals and away from the laser light and the Tell Diamond that had activated the Trinity.

The link was broken.

The propellers stopped spinning...

And the glow from each of the robot knights dimmed as they lost power and froze in place.

Dale turned around and saw a dozen spears all aimed at her...spears that would never be thrown.

"*Hoo-wee!*" She took off her hat and wiped the sweat from her forehead. "That was a little bit more excitement than I was hoping for."

All was strangely quiet.

"Is it over?" The Kid tentatively walked from the corner where he and his father were hiding. Mayor Wilder pushed past him to confront Lady Tell.

"You've made a very big mistake," he snarled. "I don't take kindly to being double-crossed."

Lady Tell laughed.

Dale and Hitch looked at each other with confusion.

"I'm not exactly sure why you think this is so funny," Hitch said to Lady Tell.

"It's funny because you think I've been defeated."

"Sure looks that way to me," Dale said. "Am I missing something?"

"You're missing the fact that there are only four of you."

"Yeah, and only one of you," Dale said.

"Not exactly."

At that moment, a dozen black-clad, bald Rivin rebels rappelled into the courtyard from the tops of the walls that surrounded it. In seconds, they hit the ground and formed a protective barrier around Lady Tell.

"We will repair the Trinity machine," Lady Tell said. "We still have the elements. My army will be marching by morning."

"Except you all won't be here to fire the Trinity up again," Dale said.

"They won't?" Hitch asked.

"Afraid not," Dale said. "Those bald boys tried to take over the ship. So I shut it down. It'll never fly again."

"You froze it?" Hitch asked, stunned.

"I did," Dale replied.

Hitch's eyes went wide with surprise. He looked at Dale as if seeing her for the first time. Actually seeing her. He let out a genuine, joyous laugh.

Dale joined him and the two stood there, laughing like silly kids.

"I fail to see the humor," Lady Tell said. "We don't need your ship."

"No," Hitch said, catching his breath. "But when you go through the process of freezing a ship, it not only shuts it down, it automatically sends a distress signal back to Sky Marshal headquarters."

"Yup, it sure does," Dale said.

"That signal tells 'em something ain't right," Hitch said. "Tell her what that means, Deputy."

"Well, it means they come runnin' to find out what the problem is," Dale said. "So while you see only four of us, I see a whole squad of Sky Marshals headed our way."

She pointed to the sky. Three flying ships hovered directly over the castle, like vultures ready to pounce.

"So to answer your question, Leonard," Dale said, "yeah, it's over."

"Well done, Dale," Hitch said.

"Thank you, Hitch." Dale walked over to Leonard and snapped handcuffs around his wrists. "The thief has now been tracked and captured. Let's bring him in."

"Let's bring 'em all in," said Hitch.

chapter 10

The three Sky Marshal ships traveled back to Alterra, one following the other. They flew in perfect formation over the buildings inside the orbiting space station and touched down at the Sky Marshal hangar only a few feet apart from one another.

The first ramp lowered, and Hitch and Dale strode out. Dozens of waiting Sky Marshals greeted them with wild applause.

"News travels fast in these parts," Hitch said.

"I suppose so." Dale's eyes were wide with amazement at the enthusiastic reception.

At the bottom of the ramp, Captain Fife reached out to shake Hitch's hand.

"Well done, Marshal. We had no idea the Rivins were trying to use the Trinity again—and that Mayor Wilder was behind it all."

Dale reached out her hand, expecting Fife to shake it, too, but the captain didn't even look her way. She frowned, trying not to let it bother her.

The three walked to the second ship as the ramp was lowered. Two marshals escorted Mayor Wilder, in handcuffs, out of the ship. Each held one of his arms.

"Fife!" Mayor Wilder bellowed. "Tell these cowboys to let me go. I did nothing wrong. It's Hitchcock's word against mine."

"Yup," Hitch said. "My word and Deputy Sweet's word. And the word of all the Rivins you hatched this plan with. They'll be more than happy to tell us the truth."

"Who are you going to believe?" the mayor called over his shoulder as the marshals pulled him away. "A bunch of villains? Or the mayor of Alterra?"

"You mean the ex-mayor of Alterra," Fife called back.

He let out an anguished cry and was whisked off to jail.

The three then walked to the final ship, where the Camarillo Kid was being escorted down the ramp by a Sky Marshal.

"You thought you were belly through the brush, didn't you?" Fife asked. "But you can't dodge the law, son."

"Not for long, anyway," Dale added.

"You got anything to say?" Fife asked Leonard.

"I ain't making excuses for what I done," Leonard said. "I was wrong. And I was stupid. It all seemed like a big adventure, until it wasn't. I'm sorry."

"You're going away for a while, son," Fife said. "But you're young. You've got plenty of time to turn things around."

Leonard looked back at Hitch as the marshal led him away. "I think maybe when I get out I'll try studying to be a marshal like you, Hitch."

"I'll be rootin' for you, Leonard," Hitch said.

"He wants to be a marshal?" cried Dale with surprise. "That rat!"

"Hopefully his rattin' days are over," Hitch said.

Captain Fife turned to Hitch and Dale. "This all came out fine in the end, but there's a problem."

"What's that?" Hitch asked.

"You disobeyed my orders when you took that ship down to Rivindale."

"But like you said, it all turned out fine in the end," Hitch said. "So it's no big deal, right?"

Fife shook his head in exasperation. Hitch was both his best and most frustrating marshal. Would he ever follow directions?

"No big deal. This time." Fife handed Hitch a small leather pouch, then walked away without looking at Dale.

"I don't get it. Am I invisible?" she cried. "He wouldn't even shake my hand. And why didn't you say anything about what *I* did down there?"

Hitch glanced inside the pouch. "I told you we

could get in big trouble for this, but you didn't listen. I told you to stay in the ship, but you didn't listen."

"And it was a good thing, right?"

"Depends on your point of view. There's a chain of command that shouldn't be broken, no matter what the circumstance is. Can't lie to you, Dale," Hitch said. "There are consequences for what you've done."

"This is crazy!" Dale exclaimed. "What kind of consequences?"

"Well," Hitch said, "for starters, I'm afraid you can't be my deputy anymore."

Dale's mouth fell open in shock. "What? We saved Tensor-4!"

"We did, and the price for doing that is you're no longer a deputy." Hitch dug into the pouch and pulled out a shiny silver badge. "You're now a full-fledged Sky Marshal. And I would be honored if you saw it clear to stay on as my partner."

Dale stared at the badge, not believing it was real.

"What do you say, Marshal Sweet? We still partners?"

Dale nodded enthusiastically. "You bet we are!"

"Let's make this official." Hitch pinned the badge onto Dale's shirt.

Applause erupted. Dale spun around. The entire group of Sky Marshals who had come to see the ships arrive had stayed to congratulate her. Captain Fife stood in front with a big smile, clapping harder than anybody else.

"Thank you!" she exclaimed.

"It's me who should thank you," Hitch said. "You saved my life down there, along with a whole lot of others. We needed you. Tensor-4 owes you a huge debt of gratitude."

"So what's our next case, partner?" she asked.

"Hold on there," Hitch said. "We still got this one to wrap up."

A short while later, Hitch and Dale landed back on Tensor-4. They flew Patches and LuluBelle through the Shadow Gap to Gilroy's mine.

"You done it!" the old prospector exclaimed as Dale handed him his precious nugget of gold.

"Now you can stop digging in the dirt and find someplace nice to settle down," Hitch said. "And you got a bonus to go along with it. Casey's yours for good."

Hitch patted the golden palomino that he'd won from the cattle rustler, Rangel.

"Thank you both," Gilroy said. "I got no other words."

"None needed," Dale said. "We're just doing our job."

The two marshals then flew to the town of Silver Spur and the Mine Car Hotel. Scarlett greeted them both.

"Never thought I'd see the Madre again." She pointed to the silver ore.

"We'll be comin' back this way to see the church you all build." Hitch held the ore out to Scarlett, but she didn't take it.

"You should put it back where it belongs," she said.

Hitch looked at the purple pillow that sat behind the hotel's front desk, then handed the chunk of ore to Dale.

"Your honors, Marshal Sweet," he said.

Dale took it with a smile, vaulted over the desk, and stood in front of the pillow. She held the chunk of silver up high so everyone in the hotel could see it.

"And now," she announced, "the case of the Camarillo Kid is officially closed."

As everyone in the hotel lobby clapped and hooted, she placed the ore on the pillow. The player piano kicked in with a happy tune.

Bright light shone in from every window. Strangely, it became so intense that soon there was nothing to be seen except white.

EPILOGUE

Gaby's and Jamal's eyes focused on the screen across the room. They were in Jamal's bedroom, sitting on his bed, each holding their own game controller.

"Yes!" Jamal exclaimed. "We beat it."

"It went too fast!" Gaby exclaimed. "If you'd

listened to me, we could have done a lot more."

"But I completed all the challenges," Jamal said. "I beat Rangel. I got the horse and the pickax and the lasso. I chose the right path out of Shadow Gap. We returned the gold and silver, and we hit most of the levels. We did it all!"

"No, we didn't," Gaby said, annoyed. "Not even close. You never should have let Patches get stolen by the Camarillo Kid, and there was a better way out of Shadow Gap that didn't involve quicksand. And we completely missed going to the museum, where we could have stopped the Camarillo Kid from stealing the Tell Diamond in the first place. And we didn't get to see the cat-people of Eelong or the giants of Prox or the invisible clans of Wells."

"How can you see an invisible clan?" Jamal asked.

"I don't know! But there are a million more things we could have done!"

"Fine," Jamal said. "Next time you be Hitch and I'll be Dale."

"Fine," Gaby said.

"Fine," Jamal added.

"It's settled," Gaby said.

"It was a pretty cool game, wasn't it?" Jamal grinned.

"Yeah, it was," Gaby replied.

"Doggit! Let's play again." Jamal moved to restart the game.

"Much obliged, partner." Gaby pretended to tip her hat, then she readied her controller. They were going back to Silver Spur.

ghost writer™

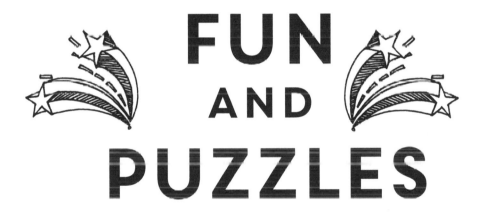

FUN
AND
PUZZLES

Things I Never Knew about the Old West

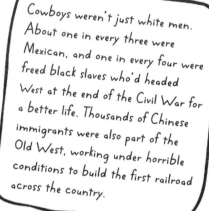

Cowboys weren't just white men. About one in every three were Mexican, and one in every four were freed black slaves who'd headed West at the end of the Civil War for a better life. Thousands of Chinese immigrants were also part of the Old West, working under horrible conditions to build the first railroad across the country.

The Gold Rush really was a race to find gold. After gold was discovered in California in 1848, over three hundred thousand people hurried to the West Coast of the United States to "strike it rich" first! Can you imagine?

Cowboys smelled funky! They often wore their clothes for weeks without changing or washing. (Sounds like Curtis after basketball—yuck.) Cowboys wore denim jeans with chaps to protect their legs from thorny branches, and bandannas to keep trail dust out of their noses and mouths. Wide-rimmed hats blocked the sun's glare and were used as cups to scoop water.

The Old West wasn't empty when the settlers arrived. Far from it! More than 240 Native American tribes had lived here for centuries. The Native Americans believed that land was for everyone to enjoy and wasn't something to be owned. But as the pioneers made their way West, they claimed it as their own, and the United States government forced the Native Americans to live on small pieces of land called reservations.

There were camels in the Old West! Yep, I was surprised, too. In 1856, the United States Army brought camels from the deserts of Egypt to Texas for the soldiers to ride. But the camels were mean, wouldn't follow orders, and spat at the soldiers. (Ewww—gross!) The camel experiment ended when the Civil War started. Some camels were sold to the circus and some escaped into the wild. The last wild camel was seen in Texas in the early 1900s.

Cowboys weren't an American thing. The original cowboys were Mexican cattlemen known as vaqueros. (Vaca means "cow" in Spanish!) They wore sombreros (the inspiration for the cowboy hat) and came up with cool cowboy words, such as bronco, lariat, and stampede.

Ruben's Who Said It?

Learning lines for a play is a part of "getting into character." Thinking about how a specific character would think or react in a situation makes it easier to get a sense of his or her personality. See if you can use the different ways the characters in *Trinity* speak to determine which character said what. Match the quote from the story to the character who said it.

1. "Those bald boys tried to take over the ship. So I shut it down."

2. "I'm the one who brought the rebels here."

3. "A rotten kid hit me with my own shovel."

4. "Doggit!"

5. "You've entered my home without an invitation. For that alone I should let my pet devour you."

6. "Come out, come out."

7. "My folks could be buzzard food by then!"

a. Gilroy

b. Mayor Wilder

c. Hitch

d. Dale

e. Lady Tell

f. The Camarillo Kid

g. Rivin rebel

Answers on page 166.

Chevon's Daring Definitions

Context clues, which are words or phrases that help the reader of a story understand a sentence or idea better, always help guide me when I'm reading. If there's a word that's stumping me, I look at the rest of the sentence to see if there are clues that can help me figure out what the word means. Or I use what I already know about the story so far to make my best guess. Give it a try using what you already know from *Trinity*.

1. The outlaw on the Most Wanted poster was a dangerous _____ being tracked by the sheriff.

      a. desperado

      b. Colorado

      c. avocado

2. If I were a _____ in the 1850s, I would have traveled to California in search of gold and other minerals.

      a. poet

      b. prospector

      c. pool cleaner

3. I ran up and down the different dead-end paths and tunnels, trying to find my way out of the _____.

    a. lake

    b. labyrinth

    c. refrigerator

4. My favorite kind of horse is a _____. I love its pale golden coat and white mane.

    a. Siamese

    b. German shepherd

    c. palomino

5. Hiking is too _____ for me. You never know if you'll come across a snake or a bear—or some quicksand!

    a. treacherous

    b. friendly

    c. fabulous

6. Oh no! While everyone was asleep, the _____ stole two hundred cows from the ranch.

    a. hacker

    b. rustler

    c. dancer

7. If I get _____ after a lot of studying for a big test, I take deep breaths to calm down.

    a. frazzled

    b. puzzled

    c. tickled

8. I walked down the long _____ that led from the school's front door all the way to the principal's office.

    a. ski slope

    b. highway

    c. corridor

Answers on page 166.

Curtis's Horse Humor

I was so surprised when we found out Hitch's ride was not a real horse! Hitch is definitely cool, but having a space motorcycle is on another level. Since I'm not getting a space motorcycle anytime soon, it got me thinking about having my own horse. I know I live in a city, but just imagine me on the wide-open plains, galloping to school. We'd go super fast, kicking up dust and jumping over creeks. My horse and I would be buddies. I'd even tell him some of these hilarious horse jokes.

What type of horse goes out only at night?
A night-mare!

What did the pony say when it had a sore throat?
I'm a little hoarse!

What sickness do horses hate the most?
Hay fever!

What do you call a horse that lives next door?

A neigh-bor!

What has two arms, two wings, two tails, three heads, three bodies, and eight legs?

A person on a horse holding a chicken!

What happens when a black horse jumps into the Red Sea?

It gets wet.

What is the difference between a horse and a duck?

One goes quick and the other goes quack.

Why did the cowboy ride his horse?

Because the horse was too heavy to carry!

Trinity is a story about perception, which is basically our ability to make sense of what we observe. Often we have good first observations, but sometimes they can be wrong. When Hitch came to town wearing his black hat and talking sternly, I immediately thought he was a bad guy. It turns out he was the hero. Actually, Dale was the real hero, and my first perception of Dale was that she was just Hitch's sidekick. My brain sure played tricks on me in this story!

Want to really challenge your brain? See if you can figure out these Old West brainteasers!

1. A woman rides into town on Sunday, stays two days, and leaves on Saturday. How is this possible?

2. A horse is tied to a fifteen-foot rope and there is a bale of hay twenty-five feet away from him. The horse eats from the bale of hay. How is this possible?

3. You're riding a horse. In front of you, an elephant moves at the same pace and you can't overtake it. To the left of you, a hippo runs at the same speed. To the right of you, there's a cliff. A lion is chasing you. How do you get to safety?

4. + = 20

+ = 18

- = 8

+ + = ?

Answers on page 166.

Trinity paired two unlikely things, outer space and Westerns, to make an awesome mash-up of history and fantasy (and a little sci-fi!). Since my grandpa owns a bookstore, I decided to search out a few more reads that remind me of *Trinity*. Most on the list are fantasy—I think you'll like 'em!

- Cleopatra in Space series by Mike Maihack
- *Game of Stars* by Sayantani DasGupta
- *The Gauntlet* by Karuna Riazi
- *Pi in the Sky* by Wendy Mass
- *Sal and Gabi Break the Universe* by Carlos Hernandez
- *Neil Armstrong and Nat Love, Space Cowboys* by Steve Sheinkin
- *Zita the Spacegirl* by Ben Hatke

When I get home from school, I like to dig into a burrito or a big deli sandwich, or even dip veggies in hummus. Between school, basketball, and Ghostwriter, I need extra fuel to keep me on my A game. On the frontier during pioneer times, it was hard to find fresh ingredients to cook a filling meal, but both Native Americans and cowboys loved corn bread. At home, we usually have corn bread with chili or BBQ dinners, and it's hard to beat. Turns out it's easy to make, too, and you can add tons of different toppings.

Here's the recipe for On-the-Trail Corn Bread.

(Ask an adult to help you put it in the oven and take it out.)

Ingredients

1 cup all-purpose flour

1 cup yellow cornmeal

½ cup white sugar

½ teaspoon salt

3½ teaspoons baking powder

1 large egg, lightly beaten

1 cup milk

⅓ cup olive oil

Directions

1. Preheat the oven to 400 degrees F (200 degrees C).

2. Spray or lightly grease a 9-inch round cake pan.

3. In a large bowl, combine the flour, cornmeal, sugar, salt, and baking powder. Mix in the egg, milk, and olive oil. Pour the batter into the prepared pan.

4. Bake for 20 to 25 minutes, or until a toothpick inserted into the center of the bread comes out clean.

If you want corn bread muffins, bake them in a muffin pan for 15 minutes.

I shared some corn bread with the crew, and they all put their own spin on it:

This is SO good with melted butter on it! —Chevon

I like gooey honey on mine! —Donna

I pile on cheese and jalapeños! —Ruben

Ghostwriter Scramble

Shhhhhh! It's Ghostwriter here with a special, sparkly puzzle. The Camarillo Kid made the powerful Trinity by combining two precious metals (gold and silver) with a gemstone (diamond). Gemstones are found deep in the earth. After they're polished to a shine, they're used in jewelry.

Unscramble the names of these beautiful gemstones. Use the word bank to help you.

NODDIMA   _____

TARGEN   _____

MERLADE   _____

HESPIRAP   _____

PATOZ   _____

OLPA   _____

ATMYSHET   _____

Word Bank

amethyst

diamond

emerald

garnet

opal

sapphire

topaz

My Mystery Word

My mystery word is a synonym for *ghost*. A synonym is a word that means the same, or almost the same, as another word. To find the mystery word, write down all the bolded letters, then unscramble them.

Here's a hint: The synonym starts with the letter P.

P _ _ _ _ _ _

Answers on page 166.

Answers

Ruben's Who Said It?: 1. d, 2. b 3. a, 4. c, 5. e, 6. g, 7. f

Chevon's Daring Definitions: 1. a, 2. b, 3. b, 4. c, 5. a, 6. b, 7. a, 8. c

Chevon's Brainteasers:

    1. Her horse's name is Sunday.

    2. The rope isn't tied to anything. The horse can go wherever he wants.

    3. Get off the merry-go-round!

    4. 13. The horse = 10, the pair of horseshoes = 4, the pair of boots = 2. BUT, in the final equation, there is only one horseshoe (4 - 2 = 2) and one boot (2 - 1 = 1) so 10 + 2 + 1 = 13.

Ghostwriter Scramble: DIAMOND, GARNET, EMERALD, SAPPHIRE, TOPAZ, OPAL, AMETHYST. Mystery Word: PHANTOM

About the Author

D. J. MacHale is the author of the bestselling series Pendragon: Journal of an Adventure through Time and Space, the spooky Morpheus Road trilogy, and the sci-fi thriller trilogy the SYLO Chronicles. His latest publication is the middle-grade supernatural series The Library, as well as the Audible Original fantasy *The Equinox Curiosity Shop*. In addition to his published works, he has written, directed, and produced many award-winning television series and movies for young people, including *Are You Afraid of the Dark?*, *Flight 29 Down*, and Disney's *Tower of Terror*. D. J. lives with his family in Southern California. Visit him at djmachalebooks.com.

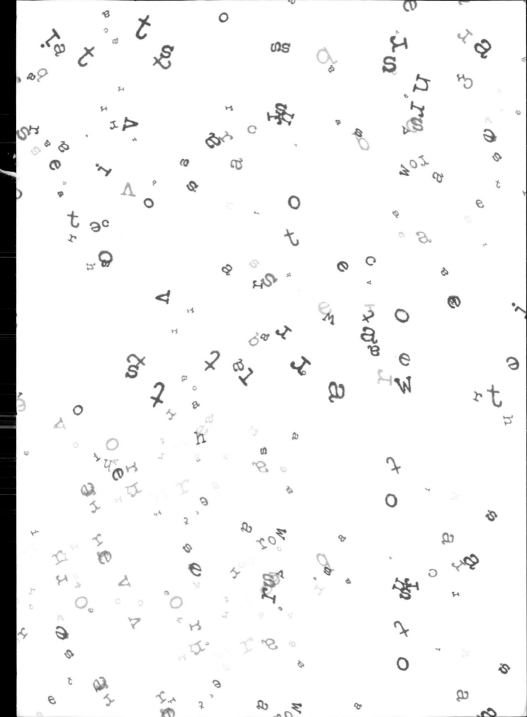

31901065582951